Geraldine Durrant & Sarah Horne

TWO BAD GRANS

To all the 'naughty' women I love - you know who you are . . .
And to Ellie, Alice and Sebastian - who keep me 'good'. G.D.

For my pals Jill and Sue. Two good eggs, and Grans too. S.H.

First published in Great Britain in 2013 by
Piccadilly Press, a Templar/Bonnier publishing company
Deepdene Lodge, Deepdene Avenue, Dorking, Surrey RH5 4AT
www.piccadillypress.co.uk

Text copyright © Geraldine Durrant, 2013
Illustrations copyright © Sarah Horne, 2013

Designed by Simon Davis
Printed and bound in China by WKT
Colour reproduction by Dot Gradations

ISBN: 978 1 84812 337 3 (h/b)
ISBN: 978 1 84812 336 6 (p/b)

Geraldine Durrant & Sarah Horne

TWO BAD GRANS

Piccadilly Press

Mrs O'Grady was a naughty old lady,
very short, rather cross and quite stout,
while Mrs Maloney was taller and bony,
and liked to give orders. And shout.

They never washed dishes,
they never baked pies,
their knitting was awful,
they often told lies.
They were rude and revolting,
said "Piffle!" and "Poo!"
and refused to do housework,
or mend and make-do.

And once when annoyed by
some small treat-or-trickers,
they threw up their dresses
and showed them their knickers.

They never darned stockings,
they always slammed doors,
their hair needed brushing
and so did their floors.

And caught out at midnight
in tangos and jigs,
they wouldn't say sorry
and didn't give figs.

They burped over dinner, they slurped up their teas.
They never said "Thank you". They never said "Please".

They grabbed the best cakes,
which they ate by the plateful,
and everyone said they were
simply disgraceful.

Ahhh
CHOO

They sneezed
without hankies,

crossed roads
without looking,

Bottoms
UP!

drank far too
much sherry,

did too little cooking,

but feasted on marshmallows,
iced buns and kippers,
and stayed all day long
in their nighties and slippers.

But then something happened
which no one had planned.
Those naughty old ladies were turned into grans!

And handed their babies, in pink and in blue,

those naughty old ladies knew what they must do.

They looked at each other, and both understood,
that when you're a granny you have to be GOOD.

So they tried, and although it was tricky at first

And then they got "better", and soon they were "good"

they were soon merely "bad" and not simply "worst".

and started behaving as all grannies should.

When eating their suppers they closed their lips neatly,
stopped spitting and swearing, and always spoke sweetly.

Their manners were better by far than the Queen's,
AND they drank up their milk, and they ate up their greens.

So thanks to their grannies those two babies grew into **VERY** good children.

Exactly like YOU!